Sitka Rose

Shelley Gill

Illustrated by
Shannon Cartwright

Charlesbridge

Sitka Rose was a big ol' gal
with hair the color of flame.
She was wild and wary—just a little bit scary—
not an inch of her was tame.

Born on a mountain near Sitka Sound,
Rose grew up strong and tall.
She climbed spruce trees to see the sky
before she could even crawl.

Rose was raised up grander than the average child.
She skied avalanche chutes for fun,
and when her vegetables needed more light
well Rose, she lassoed the sun.

Each summer, Rose looked for schools of fish,
at the start of the Great Salmon Run.
She'd swim upstream against the best,
and most of the time she won.

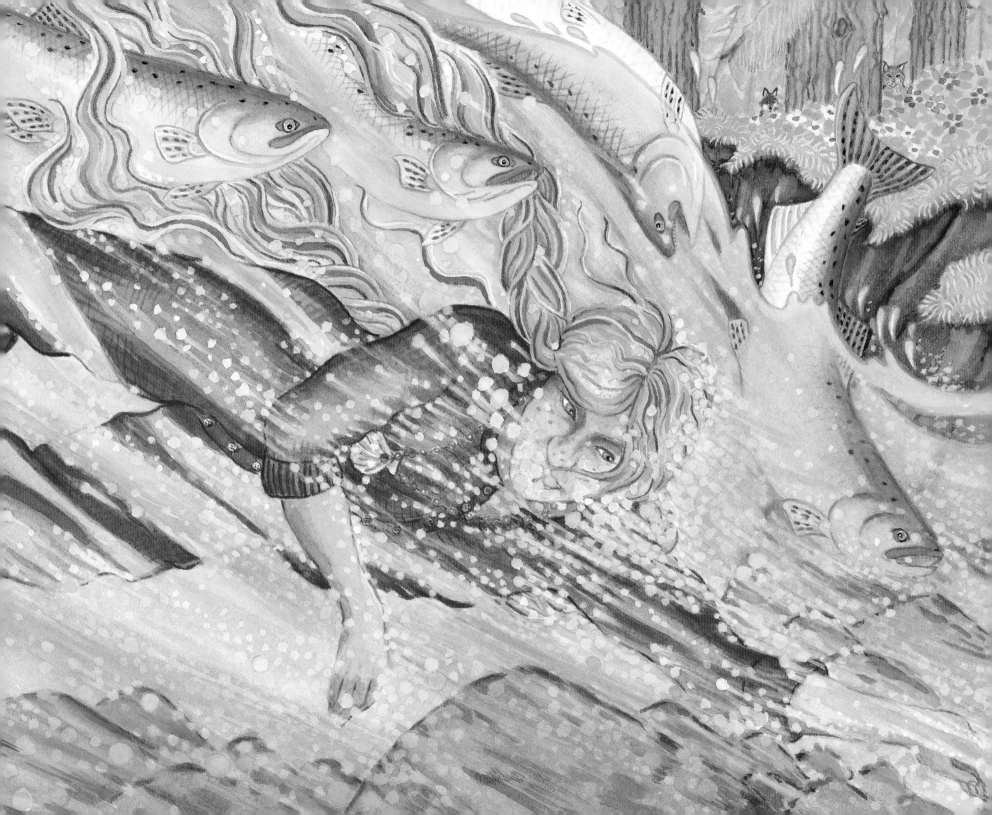

But one spring in the misty forest,
instead of worrying about the cold,
Rose got concerned, just sitting around
'cuz her toes were startin' to mold!

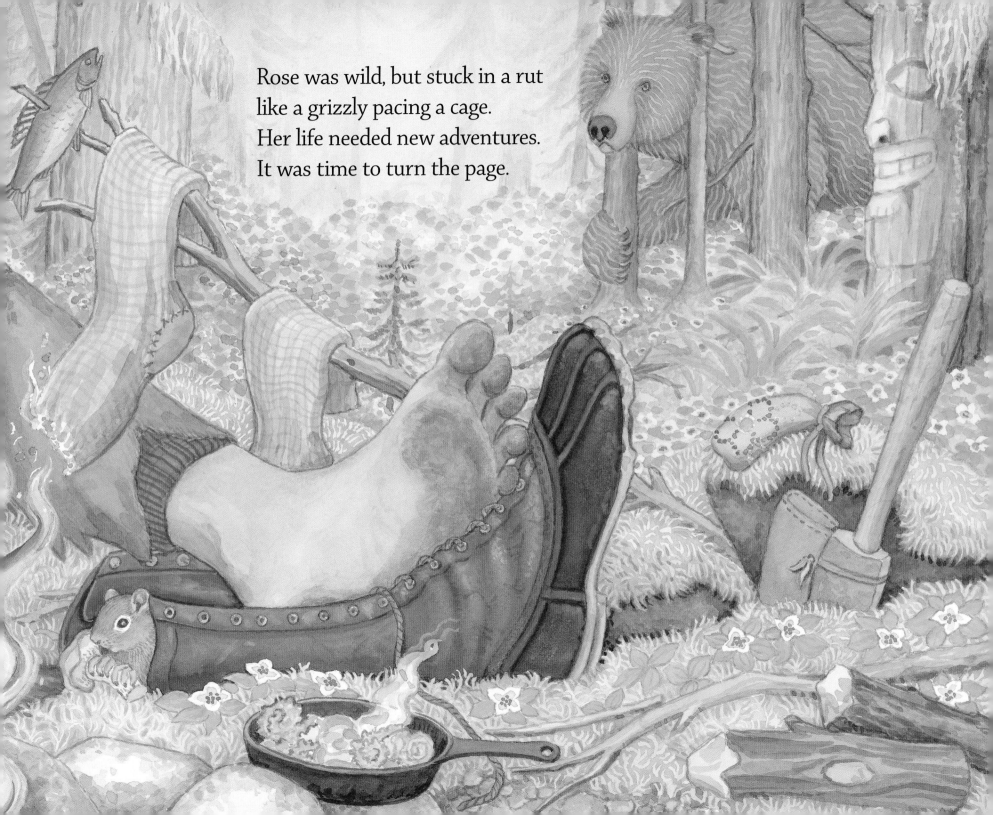

Rose was wild, but stuck in a rut
like a grizzly pacing a cage.
Her life needed new adventures.
It was time to turn the page.

Cash money had been hard to come by.
Rose's poke was mighty flat.
But Nome, it was told, was full of gold.
Rose cried, "I'll try my hand at that!"

No northbound steamer
was running that day.
But Rose spied a whale
swimming out in the bay.

She grabbed that mammal,
and hung on real tight.
The whale headed North
and swam all night.

Next morning Rose spied
the beaches of Nome,
She yelled "Yeehaw!"
and dug her heels home.

That whale commenced rolling,
flip-floppin' and buckin'.
He got so rambunctious
Rose got quite a duckin'.

The Rush was on—the beaches were packed,
full of miners panning for gold!
Elbow to elbow they fought for their share.
Men brash and burly and bold.

Rose got an outfit—shovel and pick—
but the crowds near Nome made her itch.
With her pack on her back she headed east
in hopes of striking it rich.

She crisscrossed the country
breaking new trail;
the paths caribou walk now
over tundra and shale.

Her diggings for nuggets
left ponds and lakes:
homes for swans and cranes,
ducklings and drakes.

She shoveled a trench
for what the earth could give her.
Now they call that waterway
the Yukon River.

While Rose played pat-a-cake
and pan-the-gold
she piled up whole mountains;
even Denali we're told.

With gold teeth pulled
from the Yukon's mouth,
Rose wanted adventure
before she went south.

The Alaska Sweepstakes
was about to be run—
now that sounded like
a sled full of fun!

Huskies were hard to come by,
but Rose, she needed a team,
so she harnessed up a grizzly
and ten snarling wolverines.

Nobody could pass Rose
when her team took the lead.
That bunch made up in meanness
when they were lackin' in speed.

"Hike up, Brownie," Rose hollered
to her surly lead boar.
"Yodelayheehoo, bear!"
and they started to soar.

They flew so fast,
they flew so high,
they left the earth
and split the sky.

Today in the North
Rose's legend lives on
in the mist of the mountains
before the snow's gone.

See her braids in the rivers
that flow and bend.
Hear her "Yodelayheehoo"
in the howl of the wind.

You can see her still
on clear winter nights:
dancing 'cross the sky
in the Northern Lights.

Look! A ghostly team of ten wolverines
and a yellow grizzly that glows
driven by Alaska's pride and joy:
the gal known as Sitka Rose.

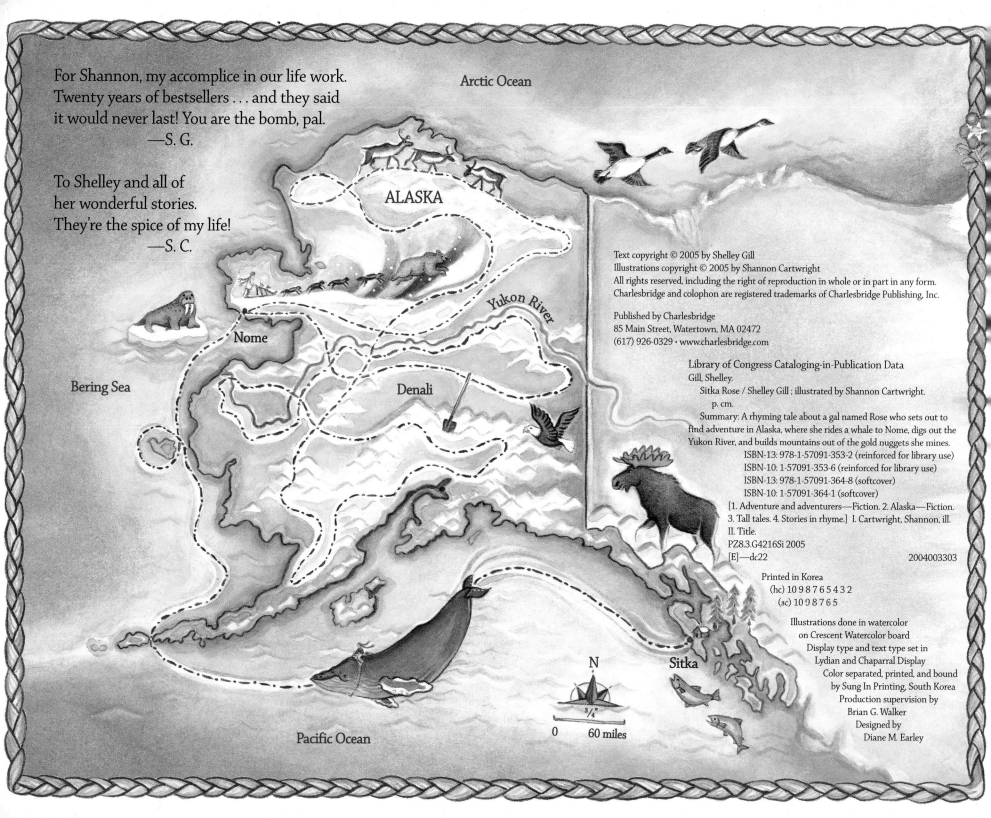

For Shannon, my accomplice in our life work.
Twenty years of bestsellers . . . and they said
it would never last! You are the bomb, pal.
—S. G.

To Shelley and all of
her wonderful stories.
They're the spice of my life!
—S. C.

Arctic Ocean

ALASKA

Yukon River

Nome

Bering Sea

Denali

Bering Sea

Sitka

Pacific Ocean

N

3/4"

0   60 miles

Text copyright © 2005 by Shelley Gill
Illustrations copyright © 2005 by Shannon Cartwright
All rights reserved, including the right of reproduction in whole or in part in any form.
Charlesbridge and colophon are registered trademarks of Charlesbridge Publishing, Inc.

Published by Charlesbridge
85 Main Street, Watertown, MA 02472
(617) 926-0329 · www.charlesbridge.com

Library of Congress Cataloging-in-Publication Data
Gill, Shelley.
    Sitka Rose / Shelley Gill ; illustrated by Shannon Cartwright.
      p. cm.
    Summary: A rhyming tale about a gal named Rose who sets out to
find adventure in Alaska, where she rides a whale to Nome, digs out the
Yukon River, and builds mountains out of the gold nuggets she mines.
    ISBN-13: 978-1-57091-353-2 (reinforced for library use)
    ISBN-10: 1-57091-353-6 (reinforced for library use)
    ISBN-13: 978-1-57091-364-8 (softcover)
    ISBN-10: 1-57091-364-1 (softcover)
[1. Adventure and adventurers—Fiction. 2. Alaska—Fiction.
3. Tall tales. 4. Stories in rhyme.] I. Cartwright, Shannon, ill.
II. Title.
PZ8.3.G4216Si 2005
[E]—dc22   2004003303

Printed in Korea
    (hc) 10 9 8 7 6 5 4 3 2
    (sc) 10 9 8 7 6 5

Illustrations done in watercolor
on Crescent Watercolor board
Display type and text type set in
Lydian and Chaparral Display
Color separated, printed, and bound
by Sung In Printing, South Korea
Production supervision by
Brian G. Walker
Designed by
Diane M. Earley